Eat up, Piglittle

Sally Grindley • Andy Ellis

It was Piglittle's dinnertime.

"Eat up your sprouts, my little sugarplum," said Primrose Pig.

"Don't like them," said Piglittle. "They're horrid."

"Well try some potato, poppet," said Primrose Pig.

"Don't want it," said Piglittle and ran out into the yard.

"I don't know what to do with my youngest one," said Primrose Pig to Gertie Goat. "He's so good, but he won't eat his food."

"He'll eat when he's hungry,"
said Gertie Goat.

Piglittle ran round and round the farmyard.

Soon he began to feel very hungry.

He went to the henhouse.
"What are you eating, Hetty?"
he asked.

"Some lovely corn," said Hetty Hen.
"Try some."

Piglittle tried some. "Yuck!" he said.
"It's horrid."

He went to the pond.
"What are you eating, Dabble?"
he asked.

"Some lovely weed," said Dabble Duck. "Try some."

Piglittle tried some. "Yuck!" he said. "It's horrid."

He went and found Gertie Goat.
"What are you eating, Gertie?"
he asked.

"Some lovely green shoots," said
Gertie Goat. "Try some."

Piglittle tried some. "Yuck!" he said.
"They're horrid."

He went to the stable.
"What are you eating, Henry?"
he asked.

"Some lovely hay," said Henry
Horse. "Try some."
Piglittle tried some. "Yuck!" he
said. "It's horrid."

By now Piglittle was feeling *very* hungry indeed.

"I've made you something delicious," called Primrose Pig. "A treat for little piglets."